FIRST
PARTY
Activity
BOOK

ANGELA WILKES

DK

DK

LONDON, NEW YORK, MUNICH,
MELBOURNE and DELHI

For Florence

Design Mathewson Bull, Chloe Luxford
Editorial Sarah Davis, Marie Greenwood
Photography Dave King
Home Economist Dolly Meers
Art Director Roger Priddy
Production Hitesh Patel, Pip Tinsley

DK Delhi
Design Manager Romi Chakraborty
Designer Mitun Banerjee
Editorial Manager Glenda Fernandes
Editor Pankhoori Sinha
DTP Coordinator Sunil Sharma
DTP Designers Dheeraj Arora,
Preetam Singh

First published in Great Britain as
My First Party Book in 1991
This revised edition published in 2008 by
Dorling Kindersley Limited,
80 Strand, London WC2R ORL

Copyright © 1991, 2008 Dorling Kindersley Limited,
A Penguin Company

2 4 6 8 10 9 7 5 3 1

A CIP catalogue record for this book is available from
the British Library.

ISBN 978-1-40533-257-6

Colour reproduction by Media Development Printing
Printed and bound by Leo Paper Products Ltd, China

**Discover more at
www.dk.com**

CONTENTS

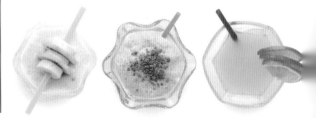

A PICTURE GUIDE TO PARTIES

First Party Activity Book shows you how to get ready for a party.
There are delicious things to cook and clever ideas for things to make.
Simple step-by-step instructions show you exactly what to do,
and there are photographs of the finished projects. You'll find decorative
stickers at the back of the book – use these to decorate your creations.
Before you get started, read the helpful pointers on these two pages.

How to use this book

Equipment
These illustrated checklists
show you the utensils and
equipment you will need
before you start.

The things you need
The materials for each
project are shown, to help
you be sure you have
everything you need.

Step-by-step
Step-by-step photographs
and instructions show you
what to do at each stage
of the recipe or project.

MAKING DIPS

Dips are among the easiest and tastiest things to eat
at a party. Make a selection of dips, provide lots of
things to dunk into them, and let your guests help
themselves. Here are the ingredients for a simple
basic dip, plus different things to add to it to vary
the flavour. On the next two pages you will find
some ideas about how to decorate the dips and
make them a fun addition to any party table.

You will need   For the basic dip

EQUIPMENT

2 bowls   Cutting board

Knife   Wooden spoon

Fork   Spoon

3 tablespoons yogurt
or mayonnaise

200 g (8 oz)
cream cheese
or cottage cheese

For the chunky dip

Half a red
pepper

175 g (7 oz) tinned
sweet corn

Chives

For the peanut butter dip

3 tablespoons peanut butter

For the
avocado dip

For the tuna dip

Half a lemon

1 avocado

175 g (7 oz) tinned tuna

Basic dip

Put the cream cheese in a mixing
bowl. Mash it with a fork until it
is smooth and creamy, then stir
in the yogurt or mayonnaise.

Chunky dip

Deseed the pepper and cut it into
small chunks. Chop the chives
finely.* Stir the chives, pepper,
and sweet corn into the basic dip.

Peanut butter dip

Add peanut butter to the
basic dip mixture, a spoonful
at a time, and stir everything
together well.

* Ask an adult to help you.

Tuna dip

Use mayonnaise rather than
yogurt to make the basic dip.
Drain the tuna, mash it with a
fork, and stir into the dip.

Avocado dip

1. Cut the avocado in half and
dig out the stone with a spoon.*
Scoop the insides of the avocado
into a bowl.

2. Squeeze the juice of the lemon
into the bowl. Mash the avocado
with a fork, then add the basic
dip mixture to it and stir well.

20   21

Things to remember

- Do not cook anything unless there is an adult there to help you.
- Read the instructions to make sure you have everything you need.
- Wash your hands and put on an apron or an old shirt before you start.
- Carefully measure all ingredients you use before cooking.
- Wear oven gloves when picking up hot dishes, and when using the oven.
- Be careful with sharp knives and scissors. Do not use them unless an adult is there to help you.
- Never leave the kitchen while electric or gas rings are turned on.
- Always turn the oven off after cooking.

Decoration
These pictures show the ingredients and materials you need to decorate the things you have made.

The final results
These pictures show you what the finished projects look like, making it easy for you to copy them.

The oven glove symbol
Whenever you see this symbol by a picture or instruction, it means that you should ask an adult for help.

FUNNY-FACE DIPS

You can decorate dips with any of the crunchy vegetables and crisps shown below. They are all good for dunking into dips. Peel and slice the vegetables carefully,* then arrange them around the edges of the dips. You can also use the vegetables to make some of the funny-face characters shown below, or try experimenting with your own ideas.

Crisps and pretzels

Cress

Sliced celery

Sliced radishes

Chives

Cherry tomatoes

Crisps for ears

AVOCADO CAT

Sliced apple

Sliced pepper cut into strips

Carrots cut into sticks

Sliced radish

Strip of cucumber

Cucumber cut into strips

Sliced celery mouth

Chive whiskers

Green pepper nose

TUNA CLOWN

Tortilla chip

Cress hair

Two-thirds of a slice of cucumber

Strips of red pepper

Cherry tomato

Slice of red apple

CHUNKY DIP

Cucumber stick

Carrot stick

Slice of red pepper

Strip of green pepper

Slice of apple

PEANUT PIG

Tortilla chips for ears

Small piece of carrot stick with cress seed on top

Pretzel snout

22 * Ask an adult to help you.

23

PARTY INVITATIONS

The first thing you will need to do is make the party invitations. Home-made invitations are much more fun than bought ones, and you can make them fit the theme of the party. Here we show you how to make three different kinds of invitation. Turn the page to see what they will look like when they are finished and to find out what to write on them.

Thin card

Small sequins

You will need

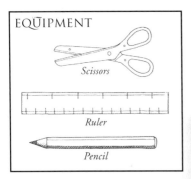

EQUIPMENT

Scissors

Ruler

Pencil

Glitter

A glue stick

Coloured paper

Coloured foil

Coloured ribbons

Cut-out invitations

Draw the shapes you want on thin card, or copy the Easter egg or Christmas tree on pages 8 and 9. Cut the shapes out of card.*

X-mas tree invitation

Glue coloured foil onto the tree's pot. Spread glue over the tree and sprinkle green glitter on it. Glue sequins onto the glitter.

Easter egg invitation

Cut out strips of coloured paper.* Cut some strips into triangles. Copy the picture on page 9 and glue shapes to the egg card.

Concertina invitation

1. Cut out a piece of paper 50 x 8.5 cm (20 x 3.5 in).* Make a fold 7 cm (2.5 in) from one end, then fold the paper every 7 cm (2.5 in) to pleat it.

2. Draw a figure of a person on the top fold of paper. Its feet and legs must go over the sides of the paper. Cut around the person.

3. Open the paper. You will have a row of people. Make a folded card. Glue the figure at the end inside the card on the left side.

Animal invitation

1. Draw large dinosaurs or other animals on coloured card. You can copy the crocodile and dinosaur on pages 8 and 9.

2. Carefully cut scales, claws, and eyes out of coloured paper.* Glue them to the crocodile and dinosaur figures.

3. Cut out the cards. Fold each in half (the head touching the tail), then in half again. There will be three folds down each card.

COME TO MY PARTY

And here are the finished invitations! Write the
details of your party on the backs of the Christmas
tree, Easter egg, or dinosaur invitations, or on the
cards with the crocodile or the row of little people.
On each invitation write the name of the person you
are inviting, then your name, the date and time of
the party, and your address. If you want a reply to
the invitation, write R.S.V.P. * at the bottom of it.

GLITTERING TREE

*Make a hole in the top of each
invitation and tie a narrow
ribbon through it, so that your
friends can hang them from
their Christmas tree at home.*

Coloured paper scales

Small sequins

Green glitter

Coloured paper claws

GREEN CROCODILE

Shiny red foil

HOLDING-HANDS INVITATION

Please come to Emrna's party on May 4, at 3 p.m. at 3 Cedar Road R.S.V.P.

Accordion row of little people

Small card decorated with pieces of coloured card

STEGOSAURUS

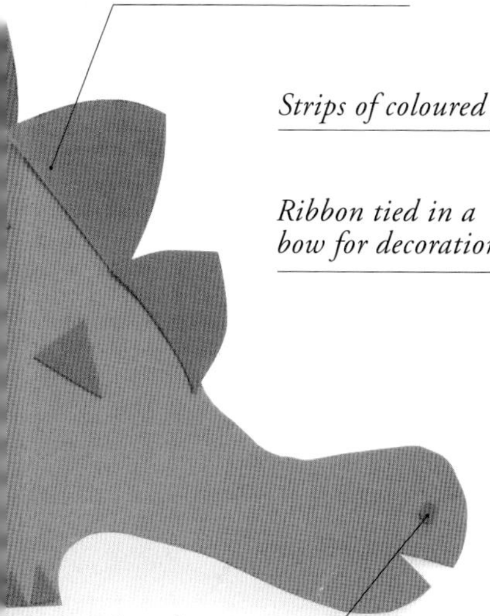

Strips of coloured paper

Ribbon tied in a bow for decoration

EASTER EGG

Triangles of coloured paper

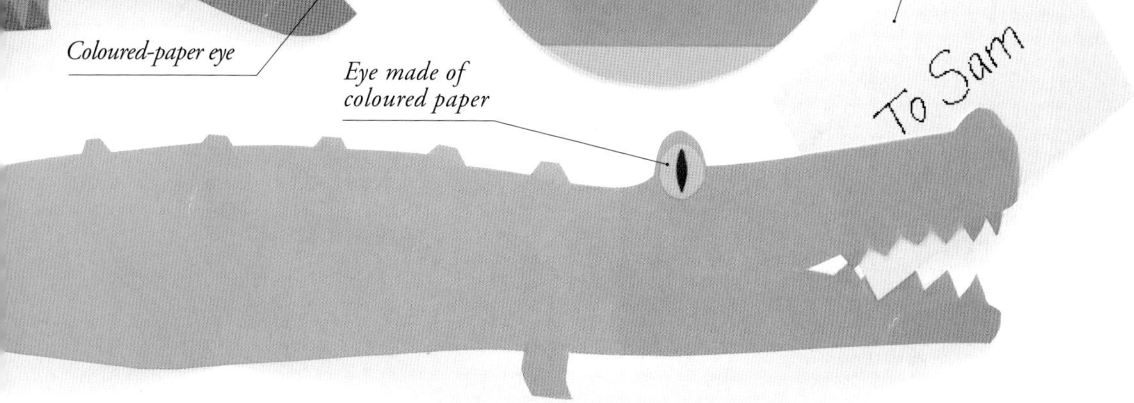

White card glued to jaws

Coloured-paper eye

Eye made of coloured paper

To Sam

MAKING DECORATIONS

Decorating the room where you are going to have your party is lots of fun, especially if you ask some friends to help you. Arm yourself with a few packets of crêpe, tissue, and coloured paper, and in no time at all you can create rainbow-coloured paper chains, giant streamers, and multi-coloured pompoms. Turn the page to see the dramatic results.

Crêpe paper

You will need

A glue stick

Coloured paper

Thread (for the pompoms)

Tissue paper

```
EQUIPMENT
```

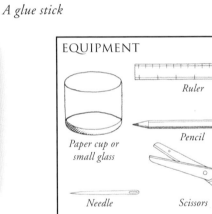

Ruler

Paper cup or small glass

Pencil

Needle   *Scissors*

Streamers

1. Cut two long strips of crêpe paper the same width, keeping the paper folded. *Snip along the edges of the strips to fringe them.

2. Tape the strips of paper together at one end. Twist them together all the way along. Tape the other ends together.

Sticky tape

Rainbow chains

1. Cut coloured or crêpe paper into long strips about 2.5 cm (1 in) wide.* To make a rainbow chain, use lots of colours.

2. Cut each strip into pieces about 18 cm (7 in) long. Roll a piece of paper into a ring and glue down the outer edge.

3. Loop another piece of paper through the ring and glue it. Keep doing this until the chain is the length you want.

Plaited chain

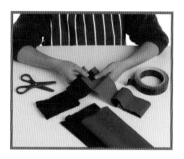  

1. Cut two long strips of different-coloured crêpe paper* the same width.** Tape the two ends together, as shown.

2. Fold the bottom strip of paper across the top strip. Then fold the new bottom strip of paper up over the strip of paper on top.

3. Keep plaiting the two strips of paper together. Tape the ends together. Then gently pull the ends of the chain apart.

Tissue paper pompoms

1. Draw circles on folded coloured tissue paper by drawing around a paper cup or glass. Cut out the circles of paper.*

2. Fold eight circles of tissue paper into quarters. Thread the point of each one onto a knotted piece of thread.

3. Make two small stiches in the tissue paper and cut the thread, leaving a loose end. Open out each circle of paper.

*Ask an adult to help you. ** Leave the paper folded, as it is in the packet, when you cut it. 11

DASHING DECORATIONS

Tape the paper chains and streamers to the walls of
your party room, or loop them around fireplaces,
doorways, mirrors, and pictures (ask an adult first).
Hang or tape groups of tissue paper pompoms
in the places where you have joined two
streamers or chains. Your room will
be full of colour, ready for
the party to begin.

CRÊPE PAPER
CHAIN

RAINBOW
CHAIN

PLAITED
CHAIN

CRÊPE PAPER
STREAMER

TISSUE PAPER
POMPOMS

13

PUNCHES AND SHAKES

With the simplest of ingredients you can create wonderful drinks for your party. Below, you can find out how to make a basic fruit punch and milk shake, and on pages 16–17 there are recipes for five mouth-watering "cocktails" on the same theme.

Drinking-chocolate powder

Frozen raspberries

You will need

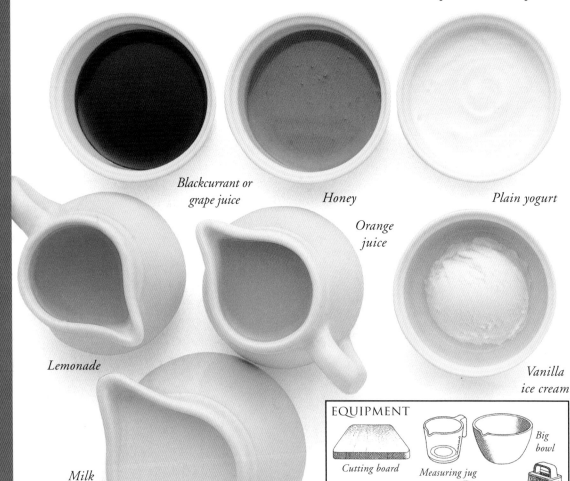

Blackcurrant or grape juice

Honey

Plain yogurt

Orange juice

Lemonade

Vanilla ice cream

Milk

EQUIPMENT

Cutting board

Measuring jug

Big bowl

Knife

Spoon

Grater

Fork

Whisk

For decoration

A banana

Sliced fruit

Grated chocolate

Making a fruit punch

1. Wash the fruit you are going to use. Cut it into halves* and take out any stones or pips, then slice the fruit finely.

2. Put the fruit into a big bowl. Pour fruit juice and lemonade over the fruit and gently stir everything together.

Making a milk shake

1. Prepare the fruit you are going to use. Peel and slice bananas.* Take frozen fruit out of the freezer to defrost.

2. Put the fruit in a big bowl and mash it with a fork. You can use a blender to mash the fruit if there is an adult to help you.

3. Add the other ingredients (as listed in the recipes for the drinks on the next page). Mix everything together well.

* Ask an adult to help you chop the fruit. 15

PARTY "COCKTAILS"

And here are five delicious fruit punches and milk shakes based on the recipes shown on the last two pages. Serve them in tall glasses or paper cups and decorate them with sliced fruit and grated chocolate. All the quantities given make drinks for two people, so increase the quantities as necessary.

RASPBERRY FROTH

4 tablespoons raspberries
2 cups milk
2 tablespoons vanilla ice cream
4 teaspoons honey

Follow the milk shake recipe and decorate with a few raspberries.

ORANGES AND LEMONS

1 cup orange juice
1 cup lemonade

Make this like a fruit punch, then slot halved slices of orange around the edge of the glass.

BANANA DREAM

½ cup milk
½ cup yogurt
2 tablespoons vanilla ice cream
1 banana
1 teaspoon honey

Follow the milk shake recipe on page 15 to make the banana dream. Decorate it with slices of banana and kiwi fruit threaded onto a straw.

RUBY FRUIT PUNCH

**2 tablespoons blackcurrant
  or grape juice
2 cups lemonade
Sliced apple and nectarine**

*Follow the punch recipe to
make the ruby fruit punch.*

CHOCO SHAKE

**1 tablespoon drinking-
chocolate powder
2 cups milk
Grated chocolate**

*Follow the milk shake recipe,
but mix the chocolate powder
with a little hot water before
adding the milk.
Sprinkle the finished drink
with grated chocolate.*

PICTURE STRAWS

You can give your party drinks a personal touch by making a special picture straw for each of your guests. Try painting simple animal faces, flags, or flowers, like those shown on the opposite page, or experiment with some ideas of your own. Write the name of each guest on the back of the pictures to make them into place names for your party table.

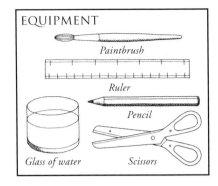
You will need

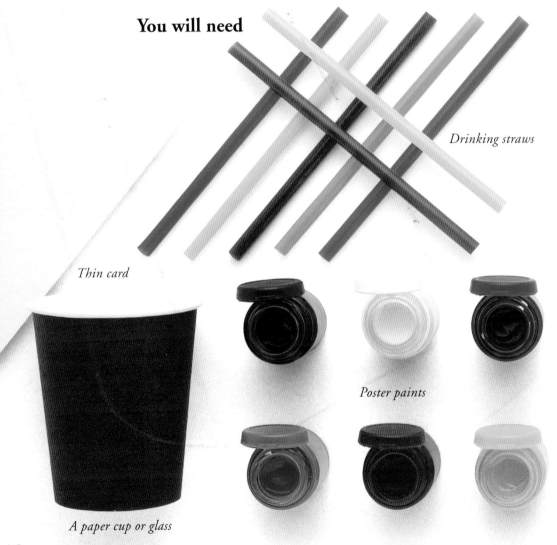

Drinking straws

Thin card

Poster paints

A paper cup or glass

WHAT TO DO

1. Draw circles on the card by drawing around the base of the paper cup or glass. If you want to make flags, draw rectangles.

2. Draw an animal face or flower on each circle, then add ears or other details. Paint them. Paint a flag on each rectangle.

3. Cut out the pictures. Using the point of your scissors, cut small slits near the top and bottom of each picture as shown.*

Finishing the straws

4. Carefully push a straw into the bottom slit of each picture, and then back out again through the top slit. Animal faces work best if the bottom slit is cut along the mouth.

FLAG

PANDA

COCKEREL

POPPY

CAT

MAKING DIPS

Dips are among the easiest and tastiest things to eat at a party. Make a selection of dips, provide lots of things to dunk into them, and let your guests help themselves. Here are the ingredients for a simple basic dip, plus different things to add to it to vary the flavour. On the next two pages you will find some ideas about how to decorate the dips and make them a fun addition to any party table.

You will need

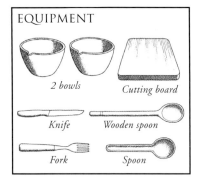

EQUIPMENT

2 bowls   Cutting board

Knife   Wooden spoon

Fork   Spoon

For the basic dip

3 tablespoons yogurt or mayonnaise

200 g (8 oz) cream cheese or cottage cheese

Basic dip

Put the cream cheese in a mixing bowl. Mash it with a fork until it is smooth and creamy, then stir in the yogurt or mayonnaise.

Chunky dip

Deseed the pepper and cut it into small chunks. Chop the chives finely.* Stir the chives, pepper, and sweet corn into the basic dip.

Peanut butter dip

Add peanut butter to the basic dip mixture, a spoonful at a time, and stir everything together well.

* Ask an adult to help you.

20

For the chunky dip

175 g (7 oz) tinned sweet corn

Half a red pepper

Chives

For the peanut butter dip

3 tablespoons peanut butter

For the avocado dip

Half a lemon

1 avocado

For the tuna dip

175 g (7 oz) tinned tuna

Tuna dip

Use mayonnaise rather than yogurt to make the basic dip. Drain the tuna, mash it with a fork, and stir into the dip.

Avocado dip

1. Cut the avocado in half and dig out the stone with a spoon.* Scoop the insides of the avocado into a bowl.

2. Squeeze the juice of the lemon into the bowl. Mash the avocado with a fork, then add the basic dip mixture to it and stir well.

21

FUNNY-FACE DIPS

You can decorate dips with any of the crunchy vegetables and crisps shown below. They are all good for dunking into dips. Peel and slice the vegetables carefully,* then arrange them around the edges of the dips. You can also use the vegetables to make some of the funny-face characters shown below, or try experimenting with your own ideas.

Crisps and pretzels

Cress

Sliced celery

Sliced radishes

Chives

Cherry tomatoes

Crisps for ears

AVOCADO CAT

Sliced apple

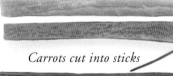

Sliced pepper cut into strips

Carrots cut into sticks

Cucumber cut into strips

Sliced radish

Strip of cucumber

Sliced celery mouth

Chive whiskers

Green pepper nose

22   * Ask an adult to help you.

TUNA CLOWN

Tortilla chip

Cress hair

Two-thirds of a slice of cucmber

Strips of red pepper

Cherry tomato

Slice of red apple

CHUNKY DIP

Cucumber stick

Carrot stick

Slice of red pepper

Strip of green pepper

Slice of apple

PEANUT PIG

Tortilla chips for ears

Small piece of carrot stick with cress seed on top

Pretzel snout

MYSTERY MASKS

Give your party a touch of mystery by asking all your guests to wear masks. Here you can find out how to make three festive carnival masks from one basic mask pattern, by using different coloured paper and adding sparkling glitter and swirling ribbons. Turn the page to see the finished magical disguises. Even your best friend won't recognize you!

Sticky tape

A glue stick

You will need

Mask pattern

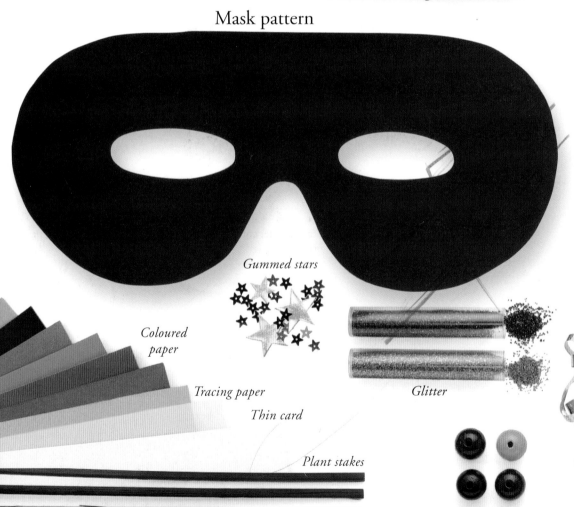

Gummed stars

Coloured paper

Tracing paper

Thin card

Plant stakes

Glitter

Beads

Ribbons

MAKING THE BASIC MASK

1. Trace the mask pattern on the opposite page onto tracing paper. Don't forget to trace the eyes as well as the outline.

2. Turn the tracing paper over onto the card. Scribble over the traced lines to transfer them to the card. Cut out the mask.*

Harlequin mask

1. Using the picture of the mask on page 27 as a guide, cut out 25 diamonds of coloured paper all the same size.*

2. Glue the diamond shapes to the mask in rows, leaving a little space around each one. Trim the ones that cover the eye holes.

Feathers

3. Tape five ribbons of the same length to the back of the mask at one side. Thread a bead onto each ribbon and tie a knot below.

4. Wind ribbon all the way down a plant stake. Tape the ends of the ribbon down. Tape the stake to the back of the mask.

Gold ribbon

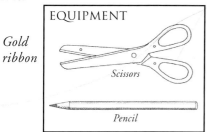

EQUIPMENT

Scissors

Pencil

FESTIVE FACES

Glitter mask

1. Spread glue over a card mask and sprinkle green glitter on top. Sprinkle red glitter around the edge of the mask and the eyes.

2. Stick on a few shiny gummed stars for decoration. Glue a feather to the mask above the outer edge of one eye.

3. Wind gold ribbon all the way down a plant stake. Tape the two ends down. Tape the stake to the back of the mask at one side.

Bird of Paradise mask

1. Trace and cut out a mask in orange paper and in card.* Glue the orange paper mask to the card mask.

2. Glue a feather to the centre of the mask, pointing upwards. Glue on two more feathers so they fan out on either side of it.

3. Cut out a triangle of blue paper 12 x 5 cm (5 x 2 in). Fold it in half and cut a small slit in the fold at the wide end.

4. Fold back a flap on either side of the slit. Glue the flaps to the centre back of the mask to make the beak point out in front.

5. Cover a plant stake with strips of orange paper. Wind ribbon over the top of it. Tape the stake to the back of the mask.

Ask an adult to help you.

GLITTER
MASK

HARLEQUIN
MASK

BIRD OF
PARADISE
MASK

27

MAKING SANDWICHES

With a little imagination, simple sandwiches can be transformed into a real party-time treat. Here you can find out how to make different types of sandwich and filling, and on pages 30–31 you can see how to decorate and arrange them to create all kinds of picture sandwiches.

Sandwich fillings

Chopped hard-boiled eggs mixed with mayonnaise

You will need

Butter

Sliced cheese

Grated cheese and carrot mixed with mayonnaise

Mashed tuna and mayonnaise

Slices of ham

Small rolls

Chopped, cooked chicken and mayonnaise

Sliced dark-brown, light-brown, and white bread

Cream cheese

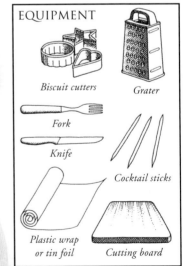

EQUIPMENT

Biscuit cutters　　*Grater*

Fork

Knife

Cocktail sticks

Plastic wrap or tin foil　　*Cutting board*

28

For decoration

Lamb's lettuce or watercress

Sliced cucumber

Carrots, peeled and cut into sticks

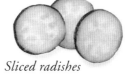

Cherry tomatoes cut in half or sliced

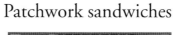

Sliced radishes

Filled rolls

Make two cuts in each roll.* Fill the top cut with sandwich filling. Arrange cucumber, tomato, or radishes in the bottom cut.

Galleon rolls

Cut rolls in half.* Spread them with butter and sandwich filling. Make sails from triangles of sliced cheese on cocktail sticks.*

Patchwork sandwiches

Make sandwiches with dark-brown and white bread. Trim off the crusts.* Cut the sandwiches into small squares the same size.

Shaped sandwiches

Butter slices of bread. Cut shapes out with biscuit cutters.* Cut the same shapes out of cheese and lay them on the bread.

Pinwheel sandwiches

1. Trim the crusts off the sliced white bread.* Spread each slice of bread with cream cheese and lay a slice of ham on top.

2. Roll the slices of bread lengthways and wrap them in cling film or tin foil. Put them in the refrigerator to chill.

3. After two hours, take the rolls out of the refrigerator. Unwrap and cut into slices about 1 cm (0.5 in) thick.*

Ask an adult to help you.

Turn the page to see how to decorate and arrange the sandwiches.

SANDWICH BONANZA

And here are the finished sandwiches and rolls
with some ideas on how to decorate and lay them
out on your party table. Arrange small filled rolls
to look like a hungry caterpillar wriggling across
a plate, complete with legs and antennae. Scatter
animal sandwiches on a meadow made from
shredded lettuce, and create a patchwork
quilt of tiny brown and white sandwiches.
Your guests won't know what to eat first!

*Antennae made
from cherry
tomatoes on
cocktail sticks*

*Cheese and
carrot filling*

MUNCHING
CATERPILLAR

*Watercress or
lamb's lettuce*

BUTTERFLY
SANDWICH

Cress

*Sliced tomato
and cucumber*

Strip of tomato

Sliced radishes

GALLEON ROLLS

*Sail made from
slice of cheese
on cocktail stick*

*Shredded
lettuce*

*Egg mayonnaise
filling*

CHEESY PIG
SANDWICHES

Legs made from carrot sticks

Chicken filling

Sliced radishes

Tuna filling

Sliced tomato and cucumber

Chicken filling

Sliced radish and cucumber

Cheese and carrot filling

PINWHEEL SANDWICHES

Sandwich made with white bread

Dark brown bread sandwich

PATCHWORK SANDWICHES

BUTTERY BISCUITS

Homemade biscuits are quick and easy to make and taste
far better than any you buy. Below is a recipe for delicious,
buttery shortbread biscuits. You can make plain, lemon,
or chocolate ones. The ingredients shown will make 15–20
biscuits, depending on the size of your biscuit cutters.
Turn the page for ideas on how to decorate your biscuits.

You will need

50 g (2 oz)
caster sugar

100 g (4 oz)
softened butter

150 g (6 oz)
plain flour

WHAT TO DO

1. With an adult's help, set the
oven at 170°C/325°F/Gas Mark
3. Rub butter over the baking
tray to stop the biscuits sticking.

2. Put the butter and sugar in
the mixing bowl. Beat together
with a wooden spoon until the
mixture is soft and creamy.

3. Sift the flour. Add the cocoa
powder or lemon rind if desired.
Mix, then make a ball of dough
with your hands.*

32

* If the mixture seems too crumbly, add a teaspoon or two of water.

EQUIPMENT

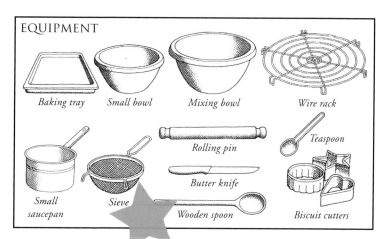

Baking tray · Small bowl · Mixing bowl · Wire rack

Small saucepan · Sieve · Rolling pin · Butter knife · Wooden spoon · Teaspoon · Biscuit cutters

For chocolate cookies

For lemon cookies

25 g (1 oz) cocoa powder to replace 25 g (1 oz) of the flour you use.

2 teaspoons finely grated lemon rind

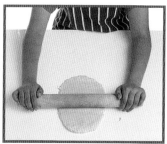

4. Sprinkle flour on the table and rolling pin. Roll out the dough until about 5 mm (¼ in) thick. Press it with your hands if it cracks.

5. Cut the dough into shapes and lift them onto the baking tray.** Gather up any scraps of dough left and roll them out again.

6. You can decorate some biscuits now (see next page). Bake for 15–20 minutes, then place on a wire rack to cool.**

*** Ask an adult to help you.* 33

SWEET TREATS

You can decorate biscuits before they are cooked by pressing chopped nuts, cherries, or Hundreds and thousands into the dough. Or you can bake the biscuits, then dip them in melted chocolate before decorating them.

Milk chocolate

White chocolate

Sugar-coated sweets

For decoration you will need

Walnuts

Glacé cherries

Chocolate vermicelli

Hundreds and thousands

CHOCOLATE COVERING

1. Break chocolate into a bowl.* Ask an adult to help you heat water in a saucepan over a low heat until it starts to bubble.

2. Stand the bowl over the saucepan over a low heat. Gently stir the chocolate with a wooden spoon until it has melted.

3. When the biscuits are cool, dip them in the chocolate or spoon chocolate onto them and spread it out with a knife.

NUTTY BISCUITS

Biscuits decorated with chopped walnuts before being baked

CHERRY BISCUITS

Biscuits with chopped glacé cherries pressed into them

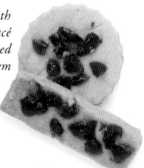

34

AEROPLANE BISCUITS

White chocolate sprinkled with Hundreds and thousands

Milk chocolate sprinkled with chocolate vermicelli

FINGER BISCUITS

Bar-shaped plain and chocolate biscuits with each end dipped in melted chocolate

HEART BISCUIT

Hundreds and thousands

DOG AND CAT BISCUITS

Eye made from dot of melted chocolate

Chocolate biscuit dipped in white chocolate

Circle of melted white chocolate on chocolate flavored biscuit; sugar-covered centre

Paws dipped in melted chocolate

FAIRY STAR

TRAFFIC LIGHT

CHOCOLATE STAR

Melted chocolate

Hundreds and thousands

Sugar-coated sweets

If using two different types of chocolate, break them into separate bowls.

PARTY HATS

If you are going to a fancy-dress party or a party with a theme, you can create magnificent hats with the simplest materials. Below we show you how to make a crown, a headband, and a cone-shaped hat. On pages 38–39 you will find ideas on how to decorate them, and on pages 40–41 you can see the spectacular results.

You will need

Sticky tape

A glue stick

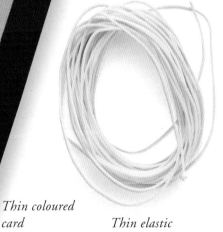

Thin coloured card

Thin elastic

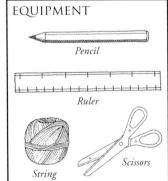

EQUIPMENT

Pencil

Ruler

String

Scissors

Cone hat

1. Draw a big circle on a sheet of card, using a pencil tied to the end of a piece of string. Cut out the circle.*

2. Cut a slit to the centre of the circle. Slide one edge of the slit over the other to make a cone. Glue down the top edge.

3. Make one hole on each side of the hat.* Thread elastic with a knot at one end through the holes. Tie a knot in the other end.

Crown

1. On gold card measure out and draw a strip about 58 x 6 cm (23 x 2½ in). Carefully cut out the strip of card.*

2. Cut triangles about 5 cm (2 in) deep out of the top edge of the piece of card. They should all be the same size.

3. Bend the strip of card into a crown. Overlap the edges and tape them together on the inside of the crown.

Headband

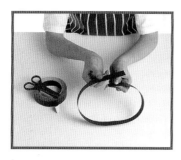

1. Cut out a piece of card about 60 x 6 cm (24 x 2½ in).* Bend it into a band that fits your head and tape the ends.

2. For a fancy crown, make a gold band. Cut two strips of card 30 x 2 cm (12 x ¾ in). Make folds 6 cm (2½ in) from the ends.

3. Tape the two strips of card to the inside of the headband so that they cross each other above the centre of it.

Ask an adult to help you.

FANCY HATS

Here you can find out how to create five colourful hats and headdresses simply by decorating the hats you learned how to make on pages 36 and 37 in different ways.

Purple tissue paper

You will need

Thick coloured paper and black paper

Gold and silver paper

Shiny sweet wrappers

Small, round sugar-covered sweets

Cotton wool

King's crown

1. Make a headband-crown. Cut out two strips of gold cardboard 15 x 1.5 cm (6 x 0.5 in). Glue them into two overlapping rings.

2. Glue the gold rings to the top of the crown. Push a folded piece of purple tissue paper up into the crown and glue it in place.

3. Glue cotton wool around the base of the crown. Glue on tiny pieces of black paper. Glue sweetie jewels to the crown.

Crinkly shredded tissue paper

Thin ribbons

Indian headdress

1. Make a red headband. Cut out triangles the same size from different-coloured paper.* Glue them around the headband.

2. Cut out feathers from folded coloured paper, copying those in the picture on page 40. Tape them inside the headband.

Princess's crown

Wizard's hat

1. Make a crown and glue a ribbon around its base. Cut out circles of coloured paper.* Glue them to the points of the crown.

2. Cover some small candies with shiny candy wrappers so they look like jewels. Glue them to the crown and the points on top.

1. Make a tall cone hat from dark blue card. Cut stars and moons out of gold and silver paper and glue them to the hat.

Clown's hat

2. Tape some thin ribbons to the top of the hat. Tape gold and silver stars and moons to the ends of the ribbons.

1. Make a yellow cone hat. Cut out two pink paper circles and glue them to the hat.* Glue small blue circles on top of them.

2. Tape a tuft of crinkly shredded tissue paper to the top of the hat and two larger tufts to the base, one at each side.

*Ask an adult to help you. 39

ON PARADE

These hats will transform you into the characters of your dreams! Raid the dressing-up box to find the right clothes to wear with your hat, or drape yourself in a large piece of fabric which can act as regal robes or a wizard's cloak.

CLOWN'S HAT

Circle of pink paper

Circle of blue paper glued on to circle of pink paper

Shredded tissue paper

INDIAN HEADDRESS

Feather made from coloured paper

Thin ribbons

Triangle of coloured paper

PRINCESS'S CROWN

Jewel made of sweet wrapped in shiny foil wrapper

Sweetie jewel

Ribbon

KING'S CROWN

Rings made from gold card

Purple tissue paper

Sweetie jewel

Fur made from cotton wool

Small pieces of black paper

WIZARD'S HAT

Moons and stars cut out of gold and silver paper

SPECIAL CHOCOLATE CAKE

You will need

3 tablespoons cocoa powder

The most important feature of any party food is the cake, so here is a recipe for a moist, dark chocolate cake that you will be proud to place on the table. The quantities given below are enough to make one 18 cm (8 in) layer cake and about 12 cupcakes, some of which you will need for the cake. Turn the page to see how to ice and decorate the cake in a special way.

EQUIPMENT

Pastry brush

2 non-stick 18 cm (7 in) shallow cake tins

Fork or whisk

Palette knife

2 mixing bowls

Wooden spoon

Teaspoon

Sieve

A bun tin or individual tins

Wire rack

225 g (9 oz) plain flour

MAKING THE CAKE

1. Preheat the oven to 180°C/ 325°F/Gas Mark 3. Brush some oil around the insides of the two cake tins and the bun tin.

2. Sift the flour, baking powder, cocoa powder, bicarbonate of soda, and sugar into one mixing bowl. Mix together well.

3. Break the eggs into another bowl and beat well. Add the treacle, vegetable oil, and milk and whisk everything together.

225 ml (³/₈ pt)
warm milk

175 g (7 oz)
caster sugar

3 medium eggs, beaten

225 ml (³/₈ pt)
vegetable oil

1½ teaspoons baking powder

1½ teaspoons bicarbonate
of soda

3 tablespoons
black treacle

4. Make a hollow in the flour mixture. Pour the egg and treacle mixture into the hollow and stir everything together well.

5. Pour about a third of the cake mixture into each cake tin and smooth it level. Pour the rest into the muffin tin.

6. Ask an adult to help you bake cakes for 20–25 min. and cupcakes for 10 min. until they feel springy. Cool on a wire rack.

THE BIRTHDAY CAKE

The finished chocolate cake is filled and iced with chocolate butter icing. The sides of the cake are coated in grated chocolate. Follow the instructions below to find out what to do, then copy the picture on the opposite page to decorate the cake and transform it into a charming funny-face bear.

200 g (8 oz) icing sugar

You will need

1 tablespoon cocoa powder

200 g (8 oz) softened butter

2 tablespoons jam

Grated milk and white chocolate

ICING THE CAKE

1. Beat the butter in a bowl until soft and creamy. Sift in the sugar and cocoa powder. Add a little water and mix well.

2. Spread a third of the icing on one cake. Put the other cake on top and spread another third of the icing over it.

3. Spread a thin layer of jam all around the sides of the cake. Carefully pat on grated chocolate until the sides are covered.

4. Use four cupcakes for the bear's ears. Ice them and coat the sides with jam and grated chocolate, as with the big cake.

Things for decoration

Milk and white chocolate buttons

Licorice sweets

Chopped nuts

Two dark sugar-coated sweets

A glacé cherry

Chocolate buttons

Cut off a third of each iced cupcake. Stick them to the cake with icing, to make the bear's ears

The finished cake

Eyebrows made of licorice sweets

Eyes made of white chocolate buttons and dark-brown sugar-coated sweets

Chocolate-button cheeks

Grated chocolate

Glacé cherry

Licorice sweets

Muzzle made of chopped nuts

45

CHOCOLATE MEDALS

What better prizes for winners of your party games than
gleaming medals on shiny ribbons, each one concealing a
disc of delicious chocolate? Below you can see how to make
the medals. You can make them out of dark, milk, or white
chocolate, or all three. If you use more than one kind of
chocolate, melt each colour in a separate bowl, so that the
colours do not mix. Turn the page to see the finished medals.

You will need

Coloured
ribbons

Large bars of chocolate

Sticky tape

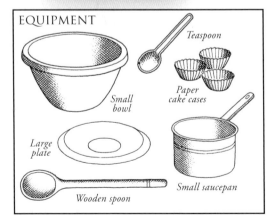

EQUIPMENT

Teaspoon

Paper
cake cases

Small
bowl

Large
plate

Small saucepan

Wooden spoon

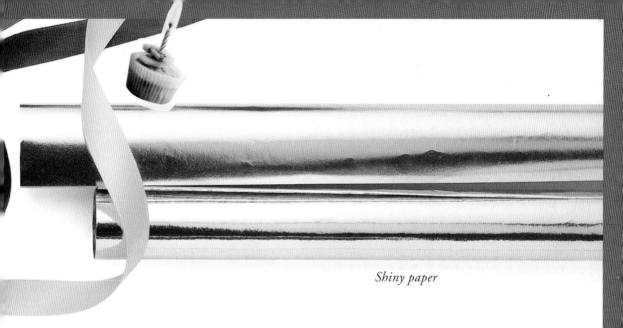

Shiny paper

MAKING THE MEDALS

1. Break chocolate into a bowl. Ask an adult to help you heat some water in a saucepan over low heat until it starts to bubble.

2. Stand the bowl over the saucepan over low heat. Stir the chocolate with a wooden spoon until it melts and is smooth.

3. Put the cake cases on a plate. Pour about ½ cm (¼ in) of melted chocolate into each cup. Put the plate in the refrigerator.

4. Leave the chocolate discs in the fridge until thay have set hard. Then gently push them up out of the paper cases.

5. Cut out squares of shiny paper.* Wrap each medal in shiny paper, taping it down at the back of the medal with tape.

6. Cut a piece of ribbon 70 cm (28 in) long for each medal. Bend each piece of ribbon into a loop and tape it to the back of a medal.

* Ask an adult to help you.

MEDALS FOR WINNERS

And here are the finished medals! They will make
good party gifts. If you play games with more
than one winner, use different-coloured ribbons to
show who has come first, second, or third.